MOUS

by Denine Foulks
with Joann Dettmann

MOUSE WORD HO

Author and Illustrator Denine Foulks
with Joann Dettmann

No part of this book may be reproduced or used in any way without the express consent of the author and publisher. This book and illustrations are the work of Denine Foulks.

Sleepytown Press
www.sleepytownpress.com

ACKNOWLEDGMENTS

Acknowledgment is made to the following publishers and authors for permission to reprint copyrighted material. Recognition is given to individuals who have provided inspiration and assistance.

"The Mouse's Tale" is from "The Mouse's Tale" by S. Lawrence Johnson, published by Abington Press, Nashville, TN, 1978. Used by permission.

A Mousetery, Military Mice Milestones, Sporty Mouse Short, and the poems, Mousezart, Gandhi, Metamousephosis, A Mouse-trick, Siamouse Twins, Crafty Mice, Richter Romance, Kilt Wear and Saint Nicholmouse are by Joann Dettmann.

Thanks to Thomas Foulks for his invaluable help and also to Deb McClain and Wanda Lane for their assistance.

Thanks especially to our parents, S. Lawrence and Alice D. Johnson and Helen and John Leskow for enriching our lives through the telling of nursery rhymes and Aesops's Fables and giving us a love of reading and learning.

Dedication

To my wonderful husband, Robert, and to all of our children, Andrew, Russell, in memoriam, Thomas, Patty and Sev, Bill, Nasha, Zoë, Piper, River and Miles, AliceAnn, Frank, Jackson and Jameson.

Each of you will find your name hidden in plain sight somewhere within Mouse Word Ho.

All of my love,
Denine, Mom, Nana

To my best friend and husband, Darryl, to our children and their families and to our grandchildren the Minnesota Twins, Jack Daniel and Grace Lynn.   Joann

CONTENTS

Introduction
SQUEAKING THROUGH TIME
    A Mousetery
    Mouse Happenings - A Calendar of Events
FAMOUSE MICE
    Fabulous Fables
    Who's Who
    Thomouse
    Military Mice Milestones
MAGICAL MOUSETERY TOUR
    Mouse-ic Makes a Mouse's Heart Sing
    Mouse-ical Mice
    Mouse-ical Foot-Notes
THE MOUSE OF YORE-YOUR MOUSE
    The Mouse's Tale
    The Mouse As a Symbol
    Sporty Mouse Short
    Fascinating Facts
CAT NIP
    A Dictionary of Mousenomers
    Metamouse-phosis—Anamouse-phosis
    Mouse Jokes
    An Ode to Nurse Ratchit
    Mouseconceptions
GOOD MOUSEKEEPING
    Cheese If You Please
    Recipes: Cat Got Your Tongue Nibbles, Brahmouse Three-Cheese Spread, Merry Mouse Go Rounds, Spicey Mice Crispies, Dessert Cake, Mulled Mousekatel
    Poems: A Mouse-Trick, House Mouse, Squeaky Clean, Atomicer
    Food For Thought
MOUSE WORDS
    Nursery Rhymes
    Words-Words-Words
    Greeting Cards
    Origins and Meanings

CRAFTY MICE
    Crafty Mice
    A Candy Cane Mouse
    Artificial Fruit Mouse
    Easy to Sew Fabric Mouse
    Handy Hanky Mouse
    Paper Mouse
    Tussie-Mouse-sie
Author's Note

INTRODUCTION

Welcome to the wonderful world of mice and mouse-isms. The mouse has been around for many centuries and there is a wealth of interesting information, folklore and stories about the mouse. Mice pop up in literature, films, cartoons, and logos. The mouse is sometimes feared and certainly can be dirty and destructive, but when all is said and done this wee little creature is generally thought of as being very cute.

The words, mouse, mice and rat, and of course cat offer opportunity for fun. Come along and see what happens when these words are either highlighted or inserted into another word or into a name. Substituting 'mouse' in place of a similar sound creates a new meaning. Change mispronunciation to mouse-pronunciation and a new whimsical word and definition result. Mouse-pronunciation is not pronounced correctly. Mouse-pronunciation has also now become the way a mouse might pronounce a word, or the unique way a mouse squeaks. Mouse-isms will bring a smile. Soon you may even find yourself making up your own mouse-isms.

There won't be any mouse-understanding if you remember a mouse is not always just a mouse!

SQUEAKING THROUGH TIME

Richter Romance – A No Fault Split

Their lives had been spent together
And they managed through all kinds of weather
But it came to a halt
When they discovered the fault
That divided their love nest forever
'Though he claimed it was hers
And she claimed it was his
Whose fault is Mouser Nature's biz

A MOUSETERY

This story begins in a far away magical hemousephere or that half of the world where mice lived, in a country known as Mousesylvania. Life in Mousesylvania was difficult under centuries of rule by enormouse Fat Cats. No matter how loudly the mice squealed for mousey and shouted, "We have been here 54 million years---look it up in your fossil records." The Fat Cats retorted, "You are just as pesky as your ancestors the anagalids, who probably lived hand-to-mouse like you are doing. Now, go back to work and quit making a commousetion or your whiskers will be cut off leaving you unfeeling and lost at night."

Finally they had no choice but to emousegrate to America. They brought with them their most prized possession----their mouser tongue, a peculiar language of mouse-isms, or words borrowed from the English language and then mouse-atized for their own use.

It was a long and monatomouse trip on the Mouse Flower but eventually they landed at Plymouse Rock. Unfortunately there already were inhabitants in this land---dark skinned people who wore mouseccins. The natives however proved to be friendly enough. Before long the natives and the Mousegrims were celebrating the first Thanksgiving.

Eventually, as more and more mice arrived they branched out to many other locations such as Mousekegan, Mouseigan, Los Alamouse, New Mouseico, Mouseissippi and Mouseouri----a mouseful in any language. Some explored large caves that were later known as The Monmouse Caves and are now a favorite tourist haunt.

It is no mousetery that they never forgot their mouserland being the sentimouseal mice they are. What is the real mousetery is that the First Colony Mice are lost while their mouser tongue language lives on in Mouse Word Ho!

MOUSE HAPPENINGS - A CALENDAR OF EVENTS

Mice are extremely fond of celebrating birthdays and national events. Join them!

January: National Eye Care month. Have your *cataracts* checked by an *Optmousetrist*!

Wolfgang Amadamouse Mousezart was born January 27, 1756.

February: National Children's Dental Health Month. Make your child an appointment with a *Rodentist*!

A rodentist is DDS or DMD. But, you see Both treat conditions of the oral *Cat-vity*.
The birth of *'Zero' Mousetel* occurred on the 28th of February in 1915. See 'Fiddler on the Roof' to honor him.

March: *Mouser Earth Day.* This day is for recognizing the ecosystem of the world of mice.
Sing "Route 66" to celebrate the birth of the *Ford Mousetang* in March 1964.

April: National Coin Week. Honor your local *numousematist* by coining a phrase.

April: In April the *Boston Mouseathon* takes place in *Mouseachusetts*.
April showers bring twenty-six milers!

To Boston on Patriot's Day they have come
Since 1897 to make this *Mouseathon* Run.

The birth of *Thomouse Jefferson* was on April 13, 1743. Go Prez Number Three!

May: Memorial Day, *Mouser's Day* and *Mouser Goose Day* all are in the Merry Month of May!
Thomouse Gainsborough was born May 14, 1727. Currently Gainsborough Paint by Number Portrait kits are available only for select mice and aristocats.

June: *International Mouser's Peace Day.*
Thomouse Mann's birthday is June 6, 1875. This patriotic mouse wrote about some very *Nazity Cats* while he was in exile.

July: Independence Day. Happy Birthday to all Mice! National Ice Cream Day. Have a *Chocolate Mousemallow* or a *Cheesecake Brownie* ice cream cone. Yum!
Cat Stevens enters the world on July 21 in 1948. The 'Deepest Cut' comes much later in his life.

August: *National Mousetard Day.* Does anyone have a Clue why the Colonel is recognized on this day?

Parsley, Sage, Rosemary and Time…..
The spice of life is not new
It is *Colonel Mousetard* in Clue.
Cluedo became Clue in Forty-nine.
A bit of logic and you'll do fine.

The birthday of lovely *Saint Mouser Teresa* is the 27th of August in 1910.

Mouser Teresa was a Saint who nurtured the poor.
Mice Missionaries give others hope and power to endure.

September: Labor Day. National Cat Health Week… Huh??!!! Cats only need one week to be healthy?
Celebrate the birth of *Grandma Mouses* on September 7th in 1860. *Good Mouseiful Heavens*, she was still painting at the age of 101!

October: Halloween.

Trick or Treat
Mice are Sweet
Happy Haunting!

October is Computer Learning Month, including how to use a mouse. Although the patent for the mouse was granted in the month of November 2007, learning the computer mouset be first!
Mahatmouse Gandhi was born on the 2nd of October in 1869.

November: Thanksgiving Day, *Amousetist Day*. All mice take a moment for REMEMBERANCE of the eleventh hour of the eleventh day of the eleventh month!
Bat Mouseterson was born November 24, 1853. This mouse never let a ratty old law buffalo him.

December: *Mary Christmouse* says, "Merry Christmas, soon *Saint Nicholmouse* will be here!"

Did you foresee *Nostradamouse* born the 14th of December 1503? *Mouse Tse Tung* followed on the 26th of December in 1893.

A *pharmouseist* by trade was *Nostradamouse*.
He envisioned events yet to be.
Frankly though, most scholars do agree
They're not true, *mouse-interpretation's* the cause.

Fall into Winter
Spring into Summer
Another year gone

Happy New Year!

FAMOUSE MICE

Deermice and a sleigh 'cross the sky they will go

Above tree tops and houses and over the snow

With gifts for all

Be you short or tall

Then *Saint Nicholmouse* shouts ---HO! HO! HO!

FABULOUS FABLES

Aesop

Children have grown up for hundreds of years hearing Aesop's fables. Aesop hobnobbed with some great thinkers in ancient Greece in the 5th Century. Aristophanes actually made one of his characters learn the fables. Socrates liked to retell Aesop's stories and good old Plato also gave his approval to the fables. Fables were not written but simply told orally. Like nursery rhymes, over the years people have retold the stories in their own words, so some changes have occurred. Although there are multiple translations and paraphrasing the heart of the fables and their messages have survived.

"The Town Mouse and the Country Mouse"

A country mouse invited a dear friend who lived in town to visit. The country mouse provided a nice supper of beans, barley and corn. The town mouse rather turned up his nose as these offerings and convinced the country mouse to visit him. "You live in a poor simple world here. Come with me and I will show you luxury and gourmet foods". The country mouse was delighted to accompany his friend to town. When they arrived the town mouse showed the country mouse a table laden with food. Cheese, dainty cakes, meat, nuts and ale were on the table. As the friends began to eat they heard a loud noise and a howling. The country mouse was a little afraid and asked what this howling could mean. The town mouse replied that it was only the hounds yelping. "I don't think I like that kind of background music with my dinner," said the country mouse. Suddenly two large mastiffs appeared. The mice quickly left the table scampering away. The country mouse then made his farewells. "What, leaving so quickly?" asked the town mouse. "Yes", the country mouse said, "It is better to eat lowly fare in peace than have cakes and ale in fear."

Being poor and safe is better than being rich and having to live in constant fear of danger.

"The Mice in Council"

This fable is often referred to as "The Belling of the Cat". All the mice met in a great council. The central concern was how to protect themselves from their enemy the cat. There was a proposal made that a bell be attached to the neck of the cat. In this way when the mice heard the tinkling of the bell they would know the cat was approaching and be able to take appropriate action. This proposal met with great approval. Then, a senior mouse stood and asked, "Who will volunteer to bell the cat?" Not one mouse responded.

If one proposes one should also be willing to perform. A proposal without action means nothing.

"The Weasel and the Mouse"

There was a hungry mouse that saw a large basket filled with corn. He squeezed through the slats of the basket and gorged himself on the bounty. When the mouse tried to get back out of the basket he found that he had become so large he could not squeeze back through the slats. Around that time a weasel came upon the mouse and viewed the situation. The weasel said, " Well, you will just have to sit there and fast until you return to the size you were. Then you will be able to get out of the basket."

Greediness leads to misfortune.

"The Lion and the Mouse"

A great lion was sleeping. A little mouse was running up and down his tail. The lion awoke and struck out his paw and captured the mouse. The mouse was frightened and squeaked and cried to the lion, " Oh, please do not eat me. I did not mean to disturb you. I was playing. If you release me I will never forget this. One day I may even save your life." This amused the lion. The lion said that as the mouse had made him laugh he would let the mouse go free. Some time later the great lion was caught in a hunter's trap. Struggle as he might he could not free himself from the snare. He let out a great roar. All the animals in the forest including the little mouse heard him. The mouse raced to the lion and when he found him said, " Stay where you are King Lion and I will set you free." The mouse then proceeded to nibble and gnaw his way through the ropes that bound the lion. Soon the lion was freed. The lion told the mouse. "I would never have thought that one day you would indeed be useful to me." "It was my turn to help you," said the mouse.

The small may be of great help to the big. You can never tell when a good deed will be returned.

WHO'S WHO

Mice certainly have made a mark in the world.
Many are fa**mouse** and having achieved great things they deserve to be noted for their accomplishments.
Many are just notorious **mice**chief makers.
Some have even been caught in a **mouse**demeanor or two.

ERASMOUSE

Desideri**mouse** Eras**mouse** Rosterda**mouse**
Eras**mouse** wrote without erasure.
Scholarly works were his embrasure.

KING TUTMOUSE

Tsk-Tsk. Tut-Tut. This **Mouse** Pharaoh went and got himself buried in an ancient Egyptian Valley.

WHISTLER'S MOUSER

Whistler created a **mouse**terpiece.
His own **mouse**r exemplifies peace.
She embodies light
In the twilight
Of **mouser**hood
And all that is good.

MOUSETISSE

There once was a Frenchman named Henri.
In his painting and art you will see
Color, form, imagination,
Pen and ink configuration.
Mousetisse; a great artist you'll agree.

MOUSETAFA KEMAL

This **Mouse** General was not chicken-hearted when he founded
The Republic of Turkey.
ATATURK is not salt-water taffy. He's Turkish Delight!

PYTHAGORMOUSE

This thoughtful **mouse** was always considered to be rather "square". He fooled everyone by developing a "hip" triangle theory.

GRANDMA MOUSES

1949 News Flash: Made**mouse**lle Magazine names an 88 year-old primitive artist as "Young Woman of the Year".
Congratulations Grandma **Mouse**s!

MAHATMOUSE GANDHI

When times are most turbulent and blue
And there is no one special or new.
Be at peace,
Troubles will cease.
Through it all I believe in you.

MOUSEOLINI

Victory in 1945! Fat Cat Fascist Benito is finally Finito at the hands of Italian partisans.

MOUSECEL MOUSEAU

Mousecel Mouseau was the Grand **Mouse**ter of Mime.
What a clown!

OCEANMOUSE

Swimming along to a tune written by the Ruler of all Water, Seas, Rivers, Streams and Ponds.

BRAHMOUSE

Count them, one, two, and three **Mice** you're able to see.
Vishnu, Shiva, Brah**mouse,** Hindu gods trimurti.

RICHARD MILMOUSE NIXON

Richard Mil**mouse** was adept at Checkers. He truly did not understand Chess very well. When he was put in checkmate in 1974, he declared, "I am not a cRook!"

MOUSE-A GRAHAM

Graceful **Mouse**-a was a **mouse**tress of dance. She brought swirling ribbons of contemporary choreography to waltzing **mice** everywhere.

THOMOUSE

Once upon a time, long ago in far away lands mice were given only one name. This was fine until there were just far too many mice that all had the very same name. Some important lords and franklins felt they should identify themselves with a surname. They were not really famous mice but at that time they were the Big Cheese and certainly thought to be the Cat's Meow. Anyway, for our story, some decided to use their father's name to identify themselves while others thought of free advertisement and began to use their trade as a last name.

Names changed. From simply being called John a mouse became John John's son or James was then known as James's James's son. Others were known as Frank Farmer, Severus Smith or Robert Tailor. Girls did protest. They objected to being called, for example, Mary John's son. Gentlemen in the Fifteenth Century did believe that surnames were 'sir names' but finally agreed on a compromise. Girl mice would not have to be known as someone's son and could be Mary Johns or Mary James. About this time mice men decided to shorten their last names too. Soon mice men were just John Johnson, or James Jameson etc.

With the advent of last names all mice mousers rejoiced. They could now pour over Baby Name books seeking and selecting just the right name for their child. Surnames opened up the way for unique and unusual given names to be bestowed upon offspring.

As the years rolled by it became apparent there is a name that outshines all others. The need for mousers to look at long lists of boy's names and their meanings can be set aside for Thomouse surpasses all. Thomouse exemplifies the great qualities of any mouse. You 'no doubt' know that Thomouse, the Apostle was a good mouse. There have been 'enlightened' mice like Thomouse Edison, and great scholarly mice such as Saint Thomouse Aquinas and statesman Thomouse Jefferson.

The name Thomouse means twin. Girl mice were quite foresighted to insist that 'son' be dropped from some surnames, because as a last name Thomouse is on a par with Thomouse as a given name. Important work and research for children has been accomplished due to the support of Marlo and Danny Thomouse! Clarence Thomouse rose to 'supreme' heights in The United States Court system. Poetry flowed from the hand of the Welshman Dylan Thomouse. Did you know the New Zealander Earle Thomouse could knock the socks off a soccer ball?

Mice mousers always want the best for their children and that includes a superb given name for a son. When they decide on Thomouse á Becket they won't find a better one!

>It is a mouser's greatest joy
>To give birth to a little boy.
>What would be the perfect boy's name?
>To ensure he achieve great fame
>A mouser knows that for her boy
>The best choice is Thomouse, not Roy.

THOMOUSE EDWARD LAWRENCE

>"LAWRENCE OF ARABIA"
>There once was a man on a camel
>Who rode to Suez to do battle.
>This earned him a name
>That brought him great fame.
>Thomouse sets men a great example!

THOMOUSE JEFFERSON

Having the Library of Congress database named for him honored Thomouse Jefferson, the third President of the United States. The acronym **THOMAS** means **T**he **H**ouse (of Representatives) **O**pen **M**ultimedia **A**ccess **S**ystem. Some silly CAT forgot to point the mouse and use spell check. The acronym should have been **THOMOUSE** for **T**he **H**ouse of **M**ouse **O**pen **U**p **S**ays m**E**! In all honesty mice can still get into the database. It just takes them a bit longer.

CARDINAL THOMOUSE WOLSEY

At one time Mouse Cardinal Thomouse Wolsey was in tight with Mouse King Henry the Eighth. He was the king's Lord Chancellor.

Wolsey was unable to get rid of Mouse Queen CATherine and replace her with Mistress Mouse Anne. Mouse King Henry was not pleased and told Thomouse Wolsey in no uncertain terms to sCAT!

THOMOUSE PAINE

In 1776 Thomouse Paine published a pamphlet. In it he wrote that it might be Paineful but Revolution for the mouses was just plain "Common Sense".

MILITARY MICE MILESTONES

Mice have been famouseliar with fighting since the beginning of time. As mousekateers they did a lot of shooting with their mousekets, using live amousenition. A lot of this fighting occurred during various wars such as the Amouseican Revolution.

Under the command of the Genralissimouse, they stormed many bastions beginning with skirmousehings to get the battle going. As fighting became more sophisticated they fired mouseiles and had to wear gas mouseks to protect their sensitive mouseths and whiskers from the fumes of mousetard gas.

Not all victories were successful and even sometimes there would be a mouseacre or widespread killing of the little creatures. When that happened the flag was flown at half-mouset for dead comrades. Not all mice were good soldiers either as some were dishonorably discharged for mouseconduct.

Eventually, as often happens in wars and in fighting, a diplomouset would use diplomousey to negotiate a treaty and the fighting would end with an armousetice. No sooner was the treaty written and signed then it would have to ratified, usually by older, bigger mice known as rats. Today, whether a mouse is submerged in a submouserine or out of this world as a mousetronaut one can count on full converge by mouse media.

Once they are back home from their voyages mice can return to the mouserland and write mouseoirs stopping only for trips to the commouseary for food and drink for celebrating peace.

ALEXANDER THE GREAT MOUSE

When all is said and all is done
Alex kept his mice on the run
Many countries he did acquire
And built himself a vast empire
Not defeated. Battles all won!

GAS MOUSEK

A safety seal used to protect the delicate whiskers and nose of mice if they are exposed to inhaled toxins. A Gas **Mousek** is not a good selection to wear to a **Mousekgarade** Party.

WILLIAM TECUMOUSEH SHERMAN

Union Mouse General Sherman served under U.S Grant in the United States Civil War. He refused to go into politics preferring to continue to lead his mice and men by remaining in the Army.

MOUSEHE DAYAN

Mice have terrible vision so this Israeli military leader as using binoculars to see the enemy troops. He was shot in his left eye with a bullet. He lost his eye and some ocular mousecles as well. He cut a fine mouse figure wearing a pirate's eye patch for the rest of his life.

MOUSEKATEER

Infantry mice just love a good swashbuckling to-do! Mousekateer D'Artagnon is quite well known but his best friends, Athos, Porthos and Aramis are even more famouse.

    Alexandre DuMouse wrote all about the high adventures of The Three Mousekateers whose motto was, "All for one and one for all!"

A MAGICAL MOUSETERY TOUR

Some music straight from the heart

For you, although we are apart

Notes happy and clear

To the one we love dear

From the hands of Amadamouse Mousezart

♫ MOUSE-IC MAKES A MOUSE'S HEART SING ♫

Come along on a 'Magical **Mouse**-tery Tour'. **Mice** are quite diverse but they all love great **MOUSE**-ic especially songs with a CAT-chy verse.

The Beatles brought us here but of course they already had Wolfie **Mouse**-zart to bring cheer.

Mouse-ic brings magic to one's soul. Are any of these songs, composers or **mouse**-ical performing artists favorites of yours?

If you enjoy **mouse**-ic or are a **mouse**-ician lend your eye as well as your ear and enjoy 'The Sound of **Mouse**-ic'!

"Raindrops on roses and whiskers on kittens…."

MOUSE-ICAL MICE

CHOIR MOUSETER

A choir **mouse**ter is responsible for conducting choirs or choruses. Church **mice** always enjoy singing A**mouse**-zing Grace under the direction of their own choir **mouse**ter.

BYE BYE BIRDIE!

Conrad Birdie is an upside down turned over version of Conway Twitty. This **mouse**-ical is a fine example of **mouse** humor circa 1960.

MICETRO

Italian mice originated this title. It is meant to give extreme respect to the **mouse**-ic mouseter and teacher. **Mouse**icians think a **mice**tro is **mouse**-jestic.

JAZZ MOUSEICIAN

Jazz is a specialty **mouse** music that ranges from blues to ragtime to Dixieland. The keynote is that the **mouse**ician improvises the key signature and the note changes as he plays his instrument.

MOUSE ORGAN

Little tiny **mice** like to play a **mouse** organ called a harmonica. Large important rodents prefer to smoke a Pipe Organ.

MAGIC CARPET RIDE

Mouse Composers Kay and Moreve said this tune was written because one liked to dream by the side of a **mouse**-ic machine. The idea of flying around on a magic carpet was later taken to new heights by beautiful balloons. Up, Up and Away!

DER FLEDERMOUSE

Johann Strauss came up with a really batty idea for an operetta. Who could predict that **mice** would like it?

HANDEL'S MOUSEIAH

It is traditional for all mice to stand during the performance of the Hallelujah Chorus. It's said that a long time ago **Mouse** King George II was so moved by this segment he stood up. Of course when he did every **mouse** in the house had to stand up too. This story has never been confirmed. It is far more likely that **Mouse** King George had stiff knees and was not moved but really only needed to move. All the **mice** then jumped up waving their arms shouting, "Hallelujah, we can finally stretch our legs."

MOUSEZO-SOPRANO

This mouse has a singing voice that is considered to be in the middle range and a bit heavier than a high soprano's voice. Well, **Mouse**zo-sopranos can be a bit heavier too.

MOUSE-EESE RAVEL

Ravel composed the very famouse ballet Boléro. How any self-respecting ballerina who was on her toes would agree to wear a bolero with her tutu is mind-boggling! On the other hand, the bolero was knit so well it never became unRaveled.

MOUSEZURKA

What a lively Polish dance this is. Chopin liked it so much he wrote sixty-nine **Mouse**zurkas for piano solo.

CHARLESTON

The **Mouse** the Twenties Roared At! It was 1923 and Charleston, South Carolina had every Squeakeasy filled with dancing mice flapping their tails, lifting mouse spirits at a time when alcoholic spirits were prohibited.

MOUSE-IK LADEN
Circa 1975

Talk Talk reporting from West German Television "Chaos erupts at Mouse-ik Laden. Several bands led by Pussy CAT and The Bloomtown RATS create Hot Gossip as they display very Bad Manners going to War over The Platters laden with Meat Loaf. Andy Gibb, Billy Joel and Janet Jackson have The Vapors watching Chilly Cherry Vanilla drip off the whiskers of The Little River Band. Sparks fly! Patricia Paay-ing close attention calls for help. The Police quickly get to the Heart of the matter. Using Blood Sweat and Tears and a bit of Clout they send Sha Na Na back to America. Mice flee the scene becoming The Runaways and are now Missing Persons.

Returning to Earth, Wind and Fire, signing off just as the Skyy clears and a Flock of Seagulls can be seen."

MOUSE-ICAL FOOT-NOTES ♪

La Mouseillaise: The French National Anthem had a different name originally. It's a war song (Chant de Guerre) that was sung along the road to Paris by giddy mouse volunteers coming from Mouseilles to join up. Mice do enjoy vocalizing!

"Mouse-ic Mouse-ic Mouse-ic": Put Another Nickel In was written at the height of the Juke Box or Nickelodeon heyday when really it did only cost a nickel to play a tune.

Die Micestersinger von Nurnberg: An opera by Richard Wagner that takes a very long, long, long four and one half hours to perform. When mice attend all hope for another Mouse King to stand up so they too can finally take a break.

Tom and Jerry: This was the original stage name of a group formed by Simon and Garfunkel. At first one was a cat and one was a mouse. They both wanted to be mice but actually ended up being quite Famouse Cats!

Pianissimouse: "Be as quiet as a mouse". This is the opposite of being very load obnoxious fortissimouse!

Does a Piper play a mouse organ? What do mice really wear under their kilts?

**Mice actually don't want to share
What's under the kilt they wear.
If it's a look you're seeking
Alas, there's no peeking.
The lad covers all with the plaid.**

THE MOUSE OF YORE --- YOUR MOUSE

Mice claim international citizenship!

Sweet Popokey ChaCha hails from Hawaii.

Beautiful Neko lives in Japan.

Pretty Gata is a native of Ecuador.

THE MOUSE'S TALE

S. Lawrence Johnson

The days immediately following Christmas are almost as hectic for merchants as the few days prior to the event. People bring back all kinds of things to exchange. You may have received clothes that didn't fit and had to be returned to the stores where they had been purchased for substitutions in the correct size. You may even have received duplicate presents that needed to be traded.

However, there are a lot of gifts you have that you can't return. How many times have you thought you'd like to trade your mother or dad for a new one? We sometimes think that parents can be problems. You might want to replace them but you can't –they belong to you. Remember the day your sister "borrowed" your new dress and spilled soda on it? You were so angry you'd gladly have traded her for Sally's sister. Recall the day your brother was such a stinker? You'd have turned him in for a new model wouldn't you? But that was impossible. He was a gift you couldn't exchange.

The gifts of God are many. Among them is that of adaptability. Mice conform to all sorts of situations. Because of their adaptability, they have developed into many species, several of which are named for their specially evolved traits. The African climbing mouse has a long slender tail, which he can circle around branches, enabling him to move easily from place to place in trees. His cousin, the pygmy mouse, is so tiny when he is born he is the size of an adult's thumb nail. Usually he lives in low bushes and tall grasses, but sometimes he can be found nesting in a fallen corncob.

The American pocket field mouse digs tunnels in the earth running eight to ten inches from its home. The Australian field mouse also lives in tunnels. He hides the entrance to his burrow with twigs and shredded vegetation completely shielding himself. The American spiny mouse looks like a small porcupine.

In Australia there are ten species of hopping mice. One is called a kangaroo mouse. As you might guess, these mice look like tiny kangaroos. Another one lives in the desert. He's not only a fast runner but can jump from side to side as well as forward and backward.

Because of the absence of ground cover, mice living in barren areas develop excellent hearing and a wider field of vision than other kinds living in swamps and forests.

These are just some of the many species of mice, each alike, yet each different. You've sung, "God is great. God is good". That is true. We should be thankful God has given each of us gifts we are unable to exchange.

Give Thanks

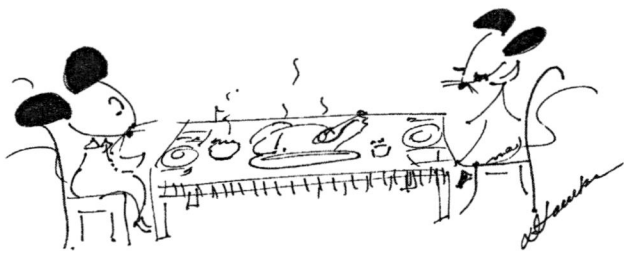

THE MOUSE AS A SYMBOL

As a contemporary logo the mouse is found almost everywhere. There are lots of church mice with church thrift stores, gift shops and newsletters named "The Church Mouse". There are calendars, assorted objects like mugs, napkins, and writing paper with mice adorning them. Films and comics abound with well-known mice named "Mickey", "Minnie" and "Mighty". Mice are found in literature. Children hear Beatrix Potter's stories, The Tale of Two Bad Mice, or The Tale of Johnny Town-Mouse. Adults enjoy John Steinbeck's Of Mice and Men, Douglas Adams's A Hitchhiker's Guide to the Galaxy and Three Blind Mice by Agatha Christie.

The mouse as a symbol has been found in early cave drawings and in medieval carvings. Many legends and superstitions surround the mouse. The early Egyptians believed that the mud of the Nile gave birth to mice and that the mouse was symbolic of timidity. In Africa mice were often used for divination. In European folklore there is a superstition that mice are the souls of mankind and slip out from the mouths of the dead. The ancient Greeks connected the destructive side of the mouse to the god Apollo and referred to Apollo's dark side as Mouse. Native Americans named the direction south, Mouse, a symbol of innocence.

APOLLO: A Greek god with many sides. One side was dark and called Mouse.

The mouse is frequently associated with religion. Ancient Judaism considered the mouse to be unclean and in Isaiah there is a warning not to eat the flesh of a mouse. Both Buddhism and the Chinese signs of the Zodiac have twelve animals, one of which is the rat, representing and connecting people to their horoscope by the year of their birth. The mouse plays a role in Christian symbolism. One story is that the devil created the first mouse on Noah's Ark. In this effort to destroy the last remnant of humanity the devil hoped that the mouse would either eat a hole in the Ark causing it to sink or the mouse would eat up all the food and therefore all on the Ark would starve.

Robert "Mousey" Thompson (1876-1955) was an expert woodworker and his primarily ecclesiastical work contains his hallmark, a mouse. This mouse is carved into the edge of all of his work and is found in more than seven hundred churches in Great Britain, including Westminster Abbey.

The term rat and mouse are interchangeable. Squeaking and scurrying mice attest that a storm is coming. Rats fleeing a sinking ship indicate that death is imminent. Mice are omens of war and are given evil and unclean qualities but just as often mice represent quietness, softness and gentleness. Mice are often a symbol of the weak overcoming the strong but are just as often associated with humility and timidity.

Throughout history mice have been disliked and feared but they have been also loved and kept as pets. The mouse exemplifies the qualities and aspects of all human nature. Today the mouse retains its popularity as a symbol as much as it did in ancient times.

SPORTY MOUSE SHORT

Mice are quite athletic and are known to have participated in mouse-olympics around the world even before recorded time. They excel at the "Pole-Cat" Vault and High Jump (leaping 12 inches vertically). They are great discus players with the Cat-a-Pult being their best event. In gym-mouse-tics they score tens on the Balance Beam by balancing on wires. Whether it's a mouse-athon, or it's sprints the race is begun, not with a ringing bell, but by a cat loudly meowing. It is not surprising that many a speed record has been broken. Whether it is in competition or not mice love the challenges of snow skiing creating small hills called mouse-guls.

Many mice get their exercise by joining a Mouse Spa where they soon become mouse-cle-bound from doing mouse-o-metrics. After a vigor-mouse workout they look forward to a mouse-sage by a mouse-seur only to discover their mouse-cara has run down their cheeks.

Come fall, however, mice everywhere can be seen watching football. All the mouse teams look forward to the end of the season games and especially the Cheese Bowl, although that could be a mouse-nomer and the pun would become a punt.

Anyway, all the mice gather with hel-mouse-ts on their heads and scamper across the field, thus giving birth to the term, 'field mice'. One might think that the field was mouse-netic the way opposites attract each other landing in a heap on or near the goal line. No matter how much they may seem to attract each other though, some mice are downright offensive, while others are neurotically defensive. One of these downright offensive mice is a mouse-sive player known as The Mice Box or Refrigerator, who brought a big chill to the defensive game, which was not cool at all, even for a Chicago Bear. The coach worked mouse-ticulously to keep anyone from getting kicked out of the game for mouse-conduct. The season ends as a gravelly, unique announcer says, "Until next time this is Howard Mouse-sell signing off for Sports Shorts. Be a good sport and don't be mouse-chievious."

HOWARD MOUSE-SELL

"This is Howard Mouse-sell reporting for the
Mouse Broadcasting Company.
And. I am telling all mice just how it is!"

JOE DIMOUSE-IO

A mouse that was a New York Giant! Really, this is not a mouse-take. Joe was a Giant Yankee Clipper.

MICE HOCKEY

Skating mice compete in this fast-paced game on a frozen Parcheesi Board. Wolfgang Puck loves it!

Wait! 'Par Cheesi Moi', or pardon me, but did you know that ever since 500 AD mice from India have been trying to bring this particular game Home?

THE RAT LINSEMAN

'The Rat' was not a Linesman at all. 'The Rat' played Center and always tried to score three goals in a single game to get a nifty Hat Trick.

MICE SKATING

A mouse cuts a fine figure by skating circles of eight in three-quarter time.

FIT FOR COMPETITION

Miceometrics: Miceometrics are exercises mice use to build strong mousecles.

Nautilmouse Mouse-chine: Mice use this exercise equipment to flex their bow. Frankly, it must be noted that while mice can gain amousezing strength using the Nautilmouse, for some reason they rarely become very good archers this way.

Mousegul: A small hill created by mouse skiers turning hour after hour on the same spot. A mousegul is the opposite of a mouseboy.

Mouseseur: This mouse is specially trained to mousesage and to manipulate both deep and superficial mousecles to enhance function. A mousesage enables mice to relax and to be in better shape for the Rat Race.

Mousecle-bound: A professional competitive bodybuilding mouse is bound to end up this way.

Mouseathon: "Twenty-six Miles Across the Sea. Santa CATalina is the Place for Me."

Mouse-ical Chairs: Mice march to music around a row of small chairs numbering one less than the number of mice. When the music stops all the mice scramble to sit down leaving one mouse to scamper away. The winner is-----The Last Mouse Sitting!

Mouse-sh: Rats travel or mouse-sh across the snow in a sled drawn by mice. When racing, mice are commanded to "Mouse-sh" and go even faster to win.

Cheese Bowl: The last game of the season. The two best teams vie for a CAT O'Nine Tails ring. Everyone then calls the winning team the CAT's Pajamouse.

FASCINATING FACTS!

Let us begin at the very beginning, which for mice is millions of years ago. Originating in Asia, little mouse fossils have also been found in Europe and North America. The history of their given name, Mouse, comes from a 4000-year-old word meaning "mush" or " to steal". In Asia their more flattering name was the "Ancient Ones". In the scientific world mice have become known by several names. These include mus musculus or house mouse, mus sylvaticus or field mice, mus minutus or harvest mice and mus musculus domesticus for pet or fancy mice. It is very easy to see that with such a noteworthy history like this, mice have quite a tale to tell.

Fascinating Mouse Facts:
- Mice are the original "Party Animals". Mice love the nighttime and feed at several places near their nest All Night Long. Mice have always enjoyed tuneful squeaking!
- Mice age rapidly and reach maturity between six to ten weeks of age. The female mouse will have up to ten litters each year. It takes about 19-21 days before a litter of mice is born and then ------ a female mouse will mate with a male mouse immediately after giving birth! The Egyptian Mouse Goddess of Fertility, Mice-is, takes her work very, very seriously.
- The amount of little children a mouser can have in her lifetime is staggering! So many children are enough to make any mouser mouse quite lachrymouse. Is the father mouse a big help? No, He is a rat! He is off somewhere else because, as you already know, mice are party animals!

It is enough to make a mouser lachrymouse!

- An average litter of mice is 5 or 6 but one litter can be as large as 13. Really, thirteen is a very bad luck number for a homeowner.
- Mice are both 'Scrapers' and 'Crafters'. Mice like making things, such as their own nests, out of just about any fabric or material they can find.
- Mice love playing games. They enjoy Hide-and-Seek and can be found hidden under things, within walls and closets and even in wood-piles.
- Most mice need a good Optomousetrist. Ah, but those mice are lucky because poor vision means they have beautiful mousetaches. Their sense of smell, taste and touch compensate for the need of eyeglasses. What a spectacle ---a mouse with spectacles!
- Mice are quite 'fleet of foot'. Their little feet can leap a foot in the air. This feat cannot be beat--- even by Ratman and Bobbin!
- The house mouse out performs all other mice physically. Mice are definitely the Gold Standard on our Planet Fitness. The most irritating thing about this is that the house mouse is naturally endowed with ability and never has to pay for a gym membership.
- Mice are quite good swimmers but only when they really positively have to be. Mice have to be in 'Dire Straits' and have their arms 'Twisted to leave the side of the Pool' to enter the water and swim!
- Rodentistry is not a lucrative profession for a mouse. All rodent's teeth never stop growing. Teeth are simply worn down by constant EATING and GNAWING on anything and everything. Mice love to mouseticate.

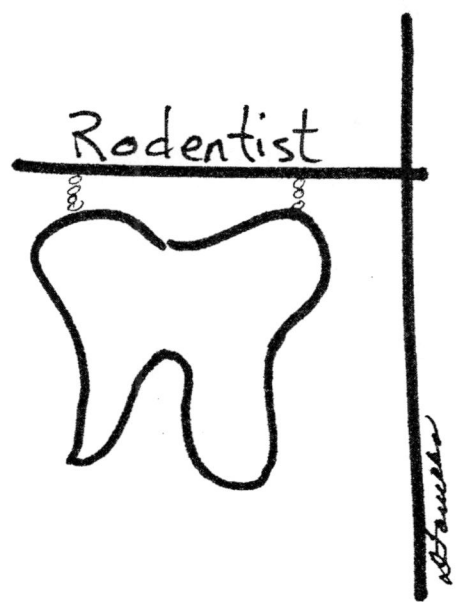

A mouse might try hanging out his shingle
But even gold teeth won't bring much jingle.

- There are well over 125 species of mice. Some species of mice work in the laboratory. So far though, no lab mouse has actually become a chemouset or even a phlebotomouset.
- The house mouse was responsible for the Black Plague that killed millions of people in medieval times. This was a Dance of Death and not a joyful Mousezurka.

Mice have talent, ability and charm. Ancient Egyptians kept mice as pets and so does modern man. Ancient Egyptians loved cats and so does modern man.

CAT NIP

Nip! Snip! Mice love sharp snappy CAT tale

A DICTIONARY OF MOUSENOMERS

ANASTAMOUSES: End to end this is the best way to surgically connect two mice.

Mice enjoy many pleasurable attachments.

MICE**B**ERG: A mass of floating mice. Detached from a glacier these mice just have to go with the floe.

COSMOUSE: A wide world of mice studied and written about by Carl Sagen. Also, this is the first name of a lead character in a popular 1990's TV sit-com.

DOMIMOUSE VOBISCUM: A blessing upon mice. This blessing is not to be confused with Requies**cat** in Pace which unfortunately means the cat got you and you're a dead mouse!

ESKIMOUSE: Native Alaskan mice that are well known for the creation of an ice cream dessert called Eskimouse Pie. Cool *cats* love it!

A Native American mouse fishing for an igloo mate.

F00T AND MOUSE DISEASE: A virus that only affects very wicked cloven-hoofed mice.

GRANDMOUSER: The mouser of a mouse's father or mouser whose ability to *cat*ch a rat is unmatched. She is a grand Mouser!

HOMOGOMOUSE: Two or more mice that are identical. Mice just like to be just alike!

ILLEGITAMOUSE: Even if a mouse has severe pain the use of mouse-juana is illegitamouse.

MOUSEN JARS: What good mousekeepers use to can fruits and vegetables.

Pickled mice have no expiration date.

MOUSEKOVITE: A COLD mouse from the former USSR.

Brrrr....A chilly Russian.

LACHRYMOUSE: An emotional mouse often moved to tears.

MOUSEGIVING: A feeling of doubt or suspicion that the gift bestowed was indeed given to the wrong mouse.

NETHERMOUSET: A mouse that lives way far down beneath the earth's surface. He's a low-down rat.

OPTIMOUSETIC: The Monty Python song, Always Look on the Bright Side of Life, is about an optimouset named Brian. Optimousetic is the opposite of pessimousestic.

PHARMOUSEY: The place where mice go to get their prescriptions filled.

A Registered Pharmouseist always dispenses safe and effective medications.

MOUSE**Q**UITO: A very pesky mouse insect.

RATMAN AND BOBBIN: The 'Mouseked Crusader' and his sidekick were dyamice heroes. Their goal was to thwart *Cat*woman!
    The 'Brave and Bold' Ratman and his partner on the alert to catch super villain Catwoman. They just keep "Bob, Bob, Bobbin' Along".

SAINT ELMOUSE FIRE: An electrical weather phenomenon named for St. Erasmouse of Formiae. St. Elmouse is the Patron saint of mice sailors.

TOLLMOUSE COOKIES: A semi-sweet chocolate computer chip set at booths along the turnpike. This allows a mouse with a transponder on his Mousetang Convertible to prepay the toll by credit card.

UNANIMOUSE: All the mice agree. They ratify the amendment.

VAMOUSE: What to say to get a mouse to leave. This is very similar to 'S*cat*'.

WAGON MOUSETER: The mouse in charge of one or more wagons used to transport freight-y *cats*.

TA**X**IDERMOUSET: A mouse that stuffs cats into cabs.

Taxidermousey is an excellent career choice for a mouse. He gets paid for stuffing *cats* into cabs and then driving them all crazy.

YARMOUSE CAPON: A red herring mouse. This is a devious way a mousetery fiction writer uses to try to cast suspicion that the innocent mouse is the criminal.

MOUSE**Z**IPAN: A quite sweet almond confection. Mice like that it comes in the shape of fruits and vegetables. They are not amused when it is presented in the shape of a mouse.

METAMORPHOSIS----METAMOUSE-PHOSIS

On a cold and frosty morn
Was born
Into this house
A *mouse*.

With her head in her hat
She quietly sat
Getting fat.

Never looking behind
She thought all was fine.
And so life passed in a blur
Until the *cat* ate her.

But my friend,
'Tis not the end
The mouse is within
With a roar soon to send.

ANAMORPHOSIS----ANAMOUSE-PHOSIS

A little *mouse* wanted to hide.
It was hard for him to decide

How was he going to remain?
But stay really quite the same?

So he employed a neat quick trick
Changing his image – *CAT*topric.

Elongated by projection
Would distort the *cat*'s perception.

What a clever way a *mouse* might
Stay hidden but be in plain sight!

 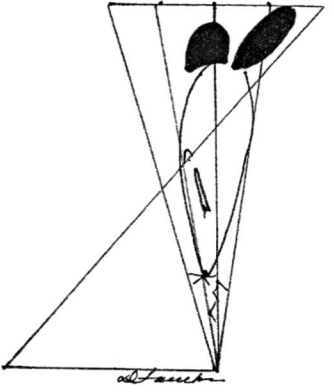

MOUSE JOKES

What is the definition of a PUN?

Pun is more correctly Paronomasia. Paronomasia is a word play that suggests two or more meanings or two sets of ideas expressed with only one series of words. So, paronomouseia is a mouse word PUN! Or? ---Is it a pun on *mice*?

- Did you hear about the *mouse* hockey player that could never get a Hat Trick?
  "They gave him a handy-cap!"
- Did you hear what the *mouse* said about the disappearing cheese?
  "I'm *mouse*-tified!"
- Did you hear about the *mouse* that was sent to jail?
  "He committed a *mouse*-demeanor."
- What is a *mouse* that uses two different names called?
  "A pseudo-*mouse*"
- What do *mice* chemists use in their labs?
  "Lit-*mouse* paper"

A chemouset tests for pH using lit-*mouse* paper

- What do *mice* use to seal packages?
  "*Mouse*-king tape"
- What kind of jewelry do *mice* like?
  "Mouser-of-Pearl"
- What do *mice* use to repel *cats*?
  "*Mouse*-th balls"
- What is an uneducated mouse called?
  "An ignora-*mouse*"

- A severe rainstorm that rains *mice*, instead of *cats* and dogs is called…?
  "A *mouse*-soon"
- What is a narow strip of mice between two *cats* called?
  "A isth-*mouse*"
- What do you call a *mouse* with more than one wife?
  "A polyga-*mouse*t"
- What kind of clothing do *mice* wear to sleep?
  "Paja-*mouse*"
- What do you say to get *mice* to leave?
  "Vam-*mouse*!'
- What do some hippopota-*mouse* become?
  "Enor-*mouse*"

AKA Mousesive. It is true that many a hippopotamouse is quite enormouse.

- How do *mice* get up-to-date news?
  "Through *mouse*-media"
- What is the line dividing the north and south of the USA referred to?
  "The *Mouse*-on–Dixon Line"
- What is a building that preserves and exhibits *mouse* historical facts and history called?
  "A *mouse*-eum". The S*mouse*th-sonian is a very fa-*mouse* *mouse*-eum in Washington, D.C.
- What is a whodunit for *mice* called?
  "A *mouse*-tery"
- What is the name of a very good school for *mice* in New Hampshire?
  "Dart-*mouse*"
- What school do mice in Virginia prefer to attend?
  "George *Mouse*-on University"

- Where does a colony of *mice* in Africa live?
  "*Mouse*-ambique"
- What do *mice* swear by?
  "E-Dam Cheese"
- How do *mice* chew?
  "They *mouse*-ticate"
- What is a favorite wine *mice* like to serve their guests?
  "*Mouse*-katel"
- What is a bipolar *mouse* called?
  "Dichoto-*mouse*"
- What did the poor little *mouse* that was not adjusted to *mice* life say?
  "I am just *mouse*-rable!"
- What happened to the *mouse* that had hypnotherapy?
  He was "*mouse*-merized"
- What is the class of *mice* who carry their young in a pouch called?
  "*Mouse*-upials"

One Australian mouseupial is the Kangaroo Mouse.

AN ODE TO NURSE RATCHIT
♥ *Thanks to all nurses for their dedication and their contribution to health care* ♥

There once was a *mouse*, a student nurse.
Her adventures now set here to verse.
Shift work or patient care,
Nurse *Rat*chit would be there!
Her motto: "Laugh! Soon it'll be worse.

**Shift work or patient care
Nurse Ratchit will be there.**

Student Ratchit did not learn with ease
The name of each and every disease.
Big lymph nodes? Inflamed spleen?
Who says what these signs mean?
Tho*mouse* Hodgkin predicts life may cease.

*Rat*chit's on clinical rotation.
She sees, hears and makes a notation.
The child has erythe*mouse*.
Impetigo's the cause.
Phooey, there's no vaccination!

One time there was a very thin man.
Nurse *Rat*chit assessed him with élan.
No fever. Just weight loss.
It was dire maras*mouse*!
Perhaps she should order a **CAT** scan?

There once was patient, Oh my dear,
A *mouset* that she defecates I fear.
For the very next day
Was her colon X-Ray.
She'll have to have ene*mouse* 'til clear.

"Let's see what kind of veins have you got?"
Ratchit asks, but she spies a lot.
Well, one 'stick' should do it.
Ten tries. She still blew it.
Clearly a phlebото*mouse*t she is not.

A phlebotomouset is a cute little lab rat that sticks mice up for blood.

The thal*mouse* gland is in the forebrain.
It's a relay center in the main.
Dare you touch something hot?
When really you should not?
Nurse *Rat*chit knows you will soon feel pain.

One may suffer from nyastyg*mouse*,
Or possibly one has strabis*mouse*.
Objects these people see
May look quite differently.
One might *mouse*take their spouse for a louse.

Mice get a new slant on life with the use of eyeglasses to correct astigmousetism.

You will see as the old wheelchair turns,
Young and agile Nurse *Rat*chit burns
Rubber right up the ramp
To reach Long Term Care Camp.
Elder care needs strong *mouse*cles she learns.

Blood pressure is hyper or hypo.
Use a sphy*mouse*mometer to know.
*Rat*chit pumps it way up high.
Patient thinks she might die,
"Please release it and let the blood flow!"

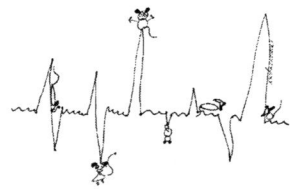

Sphygmouse is the pulse of mice life!

Diagnoses seems to be a strain
On Nurse Ratchit's poor wee little brain.
Glio*mouse*. Melano*mouse*.
Tumors? Rumors? The cause?
At this rate, a student she will remain.

When all has been said and all is done
Good student Nurse *Rat*chit is the one.
Some may think she's flighty,
But really she's mighty!
She will stay the course 'till it is won.

Nurse *Rat*chit did it. Yes, it is true
By passing her Boards she is a new
R.N. for heaven's sake!
Quite a sight she does make
Wearing white now. No longer in blue!

MOUSECONCEPTIONS

Poor eyesight is never a problem.
Mice seem to have double vision.
They can sight a double entendre
Quicker than the blink of an eye!

Mouse Trap: A device used to trap a house mouse.

The Mousetrap: A play by Agatha Christe that ran for years on the stage in London.

Mousestache: Lots of whiskers!

Mouse Stash: A pantry full of good cheese stored for the coming months.

Mouse Wash: Enjoying a relaxing hour either at the public hot baths in Japan or at home amidst bubbles.

Mousewash: An anti-CAT-vity dental rinse.

Mouseikins: Very little itty-bitty mice.

Mouseccins: Early Native American mice footwear.

Edam Cheese: Dutch cheese sold in spheres with a coating of red paraffin wax.

E-dam Cheese: What mice swear by!

Swiss Cheese: A generic name for a variety of American cheese. Its' distinctive appearance is that it has "eyes" or holes throughout the cheese.

Swiss Cheese: Mice refer to this cheese as being, "Holy, Wholly, Holey".

Cottage Cheese: A cheese curd that is drained.

"Little Miss Mousette sat eating her curds and whey."

Cottage Cheese: A summer cottage or camp for mice.

Mouser Superior: The Mousetress in charge of the convent.

Mouser Superior: Cat nipped by the end of a tail.

GOOD MOUSEKEEPING

A Mousekeeper keeps a good house.
Or is it a Cat that keeps a good mouse?

CHEESE IF YOU PLEASE

A cheese tasting party can turn into an international taste-testing event. This type of party is fun both to plan and to participate in. Preparation for guests begins with the selection of eight to twelve different types of cheeses. Buy cheese in quantities that will give everyone an opportunity to taste various flavors. Provide four different types of cheese. Include soft, semi-soft, semi-hard and pungent. Cheese that has origins in other countries has interesting names such as Brie, Jarlsberg, Gruyere and Limburger. By choosing different colors, flavors, textures, and shapes an eye CATching display can be created.

About an hour prior to the tasting party bring all cheese up to room temperature. Set the various cheeses out on different cheese boards or platters. If there is enough space use at least four serving dishes. Using four dishes allows for the arrangement of each of the four types of cheese to be displayed together. Label each cheese. A way to do this is would be to use name place-card holders (see Paper Mouse). Provide a separate knife or a cheese slicer for each cheese. Reputable kitchen stores offer cheese holders, knives and even dishes in the shape of a mouse or wedge of cheese.

For tasting cheese it is better to use mild crackers or slices of French bread. Highly seasoned crackers often will not allow the flavor of the cheese to be savored. Guests may also enjoy a piece of fruit or some nuts with the cheese and crackers.

The following guide offers suggestions for cheese selection. It notes options for fruit and wine that can be offered with each type of cheese. A glass of sparkling water with a wedge of lemon or lime also makes an excellent drink for a cheese tasting.

Before the party is over a photographer can document the event by taking a picture. Have everyone smile by saying, "Cheese". This photo will make everyone feel famousely grand!

SAY CHEESE!

CHEESE TYPE	VARIETIES	FRUITS	WINES
SOFT	Brie		Sparkling
	Crescemza		Chardonnay (not oakey)
	Camembert	Olives	Shiraz
	Mozzarella		Pinot Noir

Brie is similar to Camembert but slightly firmer and is creamy yellow with a thin brown and white crust. Camembert, when ripe, softens to a thick cream consistency and has a beautifully full rich flavor. Crescemza (Stracchio) is creamy and mild. It comes from Italy and frequently has herbs mixed in it.

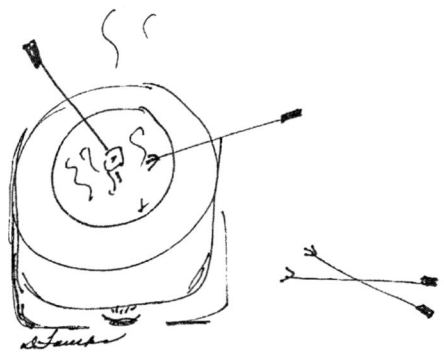

CHEESE TYPE	VARIETIES	FRUITS	WINES
SEMI-SOFT	Jarlsberg	Grapes	Sparkling
	Gouda		Chardonnay
	Chevre		Sauvignon Blanc
	Mild Cheddar		Reisling
	Goat Cheese		

Edam and Gouda are round and red wax coated. Both are yellow to yellow-orange in color, and have a firm smooth texture with a mild sweet nutlike flavor.

Cheddar, often called Rat Cheese, is a favorite all-round firm cheese. It ranges from being mild to extra sharp in flavor. The texture may also vary from solid to crumbly. Cheddar is sold in wedges or blocks and can also be found in the processed form.

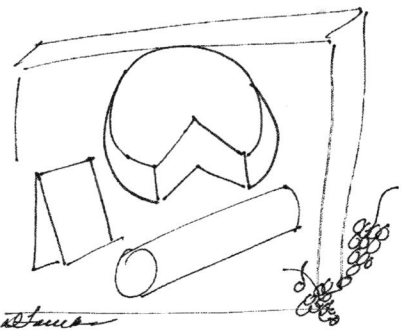

CHEESE TYPE	VARIETIES	FRUITS	WINES
SEMI-HARD	Extra sharp Cheddar	Apples	Full bodied Chardonnay
	Dry Jack		Merlot
	Asiago		Zinfindel
	Gruyere		Pinot Noir
	Parmesan		Shiraz
			Port or Sherry

Gruyere is a nutty flavored cheese that melts easily for fondue. It is ideal for dessert with fruit and crackers. Asiago and Parmeson are frequently used in making many Italian dishes including pizza. Monterey Jack Cheese is quite mild and has a creamy texture. Originally from California it is sometimes referred to simply as just, "Jack".

CHEESE TYPE	VARIETIES	FRUITS	WINES
PUNGENT	Bleu	Pears	Sparkling
	Roquefort		Riesling (fruity)
	Wash-Rind		Gewurztraminer
	Limburger		Port or Sherry

The name for Bleu or Blue Cheese comes from the spirals of little veins of blue mold that give it such a tangy and peppy flavor. Cheese-lovers relish the very pungent odor of Limburger cheese. Limburger was first made in Belgium.

CAT GOT YOUR TONGUE NIBBLES

1 package green onion dip mix
1 package Ranch dip mix (or Ranch salad dressing mix)
2 T dill weed
2 T dehydrated minced garlic
2 T dried cilantro
1/2 c oil
Mix the above in a large bowl.
Add:
1)   Two bags cheese-flavored fish or bunny shaped crackers and one 16 oz bag oyster crackers, or
2)   Two 9 oz boxes of any cheese-flavored crackers
Mix until crackers are coated. Spread crackers out in a single layer on cookie sheets. Bake for 10 minutes at 250° degrees. Stir gently. Bake another ten minutes. Cool completely. Store in an airtight container. For variety use any mixture of the above different crackers.
When making half the recipe use either one packet of dressing or one packet of dip mix.

BRAHMOUSE-THREE-CHEESE SPREAD

2 c sharp cheddar, finely grated
1 8 oz. block cream cheese
3 oz. crumbled blue cheese
1 tsp Worcestershire sauce
10 drops hot sauce
1 clove garlic, minced or pressed
1 T Port Wine (optional)
Mix all the ingredients in a food processor or use a hand-mixer. For a creamy texture whip or blend the mixture adding small amounts of milk until the desired consistency is obtained. Serve with crackers.

MERRY MOUSE G0-ROUNDS

¼ lb. Cheddar cheese, grated
¼ lb. Swiss cheese, grated
6 T butter, softened
1 ½ cups flour
1 tsp salt
2 tsp Worcestershire sauce
4-6 dashes hot sauce
6 T milk

Blend all ingredients in a mixer. Form into a 1-inch log roll. Roll in sesame seeds. Chill and freeze.
Slice the roll thinly (about ¼ in. rounds). Bake at 375° for 10-12 minutes.

SPICEY MICE CRISPIES

1 c butter
1 ½ c sharp cheese, grated
½ c Monterey Jack (or Monterey Jack Salsa cheese), grated
2 c flour
2 c dry rice cereal (Krispies or Chex)
½ to ¾ tsp red pepper flakes
1/4 tsp hot sauce
½ tsp salt

Cream the butter and the cheeses. Add spices. Add dry cereal and blend well with mixer. Add flour and mix. Form into 1–1 ½ inch balls. Place on a greased cookie sheet. Flatten with a fork. Bake at 350° for 12-15 minutes.

MICE LIKE BITS

¾ c vegetable oil
2 T dill weed
1 envelope Ranch Salad Dressing mix
1 tsp garlic powder
2 packages Ritz-Bits with cheese
1 package mini-pretzel with cheese sandwiches

Mix all ingredients together and place in a jar with tight-fitting lid. Refrigerate overnight and to store. Turn the jar over each day as the oil settles.

DESSERT CAKE

When you bake a cake, A mouse you can make!

Bake a cake using two 8 inch-round layer pans. Use a cake mix or your favorite recipe. Cool completely on wire racks.

Take the first layer and trim off the edges as indicated. Discard the scraps or… perhaps you could give them to a little mouse nearby to nibble on. Place the newly shaped cake on an aluminum foil lined cookie sheet. This will be the face of the mouse.

Take the second round layer and cut it in half. Then cut one of the halves into quarters. Place the quarters in the slots on top of the face on the cookie sheet to form ears. Then place the half round layer under the face to become the body of the mouse.

Frost as desired. Make a white mouse with chocolate ears, an all chocolate mouse, or even a pink mouse.
Make the mouse cake come to life with creative ways of decorating. Mini cookies, Peppermint Pattys, and round pastel mints make good eyes. Large gumdrops or mini cookies make a nose. Create whiskers with licorice whips, Pocky Sticks or pretzel sticks.

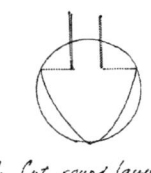
1. Cut round layer on lines. Discard scraps

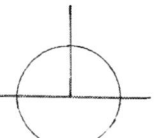
2. Cut round layer in ½. Cut one side again in quarters

3. Frost. Add cookie eyes, pretzel mustache and gumdrop nose.

MULLED MOUSEKATEL

2 cups water
1-2 tsp ground cardamom
1 tsp ground allspice
2 cinnamon sticks
12 whole cloves
½ orange, cut into small wedges
1 cup cane sugar
1 cup raisins
1 cup slivered almonds
4 cups (one bottle) of good quality Mousekatel (or Mousecato) wine
1 cup Port wine
2 Cups Brandy

Boil the sugar and water with the spices and the orange sections. Let this steep overnight. Place the raisins and the nuts in a large saucepan. Strain the spiced sugar water while pouring it on top of the nuts and raisins. Now add all three wines. Cook on medium heat until hot but not boiling. Serve warm with a small amount of the raisins and nuts in each cup. This recipe halves easily.

Enjoy having a cup of mulled Mousekatel after a day on the slopes.

A MOUSE-TRICK

Good Mouse-keeping
Is Light Mouse-keeping

My name is Larry the mouse
I'll gladly stalk any Good House--
Keeping well out of sight
Lest the cats try to bite
And all of my fun they would douse.

But one day I must openly confess
The house was truly a mess.
Out of hiding I came
With my merry maids sane
And soon the house mess was noticeably less.

So when in doubt as to where one should go
To escape from a life full of woe.
The excitement and fun
Is easily won
In the battle cry---Mouse Words we go!

HOUSE MOUSE

There once was a sweet mouse
Who did love to keep house.
She swept and she dusted.
Dust kittens were busted.
No dirt in her cosmouse.

SQUEAKY CLEAN

To clear the rubble she went to a lot of trouble.
The Mouse of the House can now relax in a bubble.
Her skin's soft and smooth like velveteen.
This mouse and her house are squeaky clean.

ATOMICER

Having had a good long soak in the tub
A mouse enjoys a soothing back rub.
Pretty, dressed and wanting to impress,
All she needs is just a spritz of perfume.
Using an atomicer is opportune.

FOOD FOR THOUGHT

Mousemallows: Delicious white fluffy confections best eaten after being roasted over an open fire. They are often served as a sandwich made with chocolate and graham crackers.
Chocolate Mouse: Unlike solid chocolate bunnies a chocolate mouse is a delectable whipped pudding. Yum!
Baked Mousekellunge: This giant fish, found in North America, can weigh from 60-90 lbs. Just one Baked Mousekellunge feeds a mousesive crowd of mice!
Mouseshrooms: Just for fun-gi a lot of mice opt for mouseshrooms on their pizza.
Ratatouille: A yummy vegetable stew. Niçoise is 'bon appitit' to a mouse.
Mouseaka: Greek mice particularly like this eggplant and tomato dish.
Mouseticate: Chewing and gnawing are an important part of any mouse's life.
Hummouse: A tasty spread made from chickpeas, lemon juice and olive oil. This is not humouse! Humouse is just the dirt from mouse-made tunnels.
Thermouse: A unique insulated container used to transport mice going on a picnic. A thermouse keeps them wonderfully warm or comfortably cool on the journey even without a thermousetat.
Mousecadine: A grapevine with small little clusters of mouseky mice.

Ratskeller: A basement tavern where mice gather to have a mouseseux drink and gossip.

MOUSE WORDS

Cat's Cradle

NURSERY RHYMES
Attributed to Mother Goose

Records of children's rhyme songs stem from the middle ages. Some nursery rhymes are said to have hidden meanings and many nursery rhymes can actually be linked to historical persons or events. Scholars agree though that the origins and meanings of most nursery rhymes are unknown. First to children and then to grandchildren, adults recite nursery rhymes. Rhymes have passed from generation to generation with only slight variations. Some nursery rhymes feature an all time favorite, the mouse.

Three blind mice, three blind mice,
See how they run, see how they run,
They all ran after the farmer's wife,
Who cut off their tails with a carving knife,
Did you ever see such a sight in your life,
As three blind mice?

Hickory Dickory Dock,
The mouse ran up the clock.
The clock struck one!
The mouse ran down,
Hickory Dickory Dock.

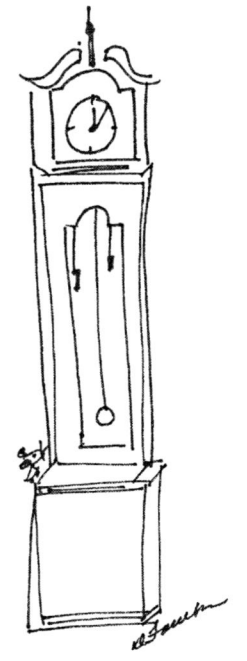

Hickory Dickory Dock,
The mouse ran up the clock.
The clock struck two!
And down he flew.
Hickory Dickory Dock.

Hickory Dickory Dock,
The mouse ran up the clock.
The clock struck three!
And he did flee.
Hickory Dickory Dock.

Hickory Dickory Dock,
The mouse ran up the clock.
The clock struck four!
He hit the floor.
Hickory Dickory Dock.

Hickory Dickory Dock,
The mouse ran up the clock.
The clock struck five!
The mouse took a dive.
Hickory Dickory Dock.

Hickory Dickory Dock,
The mouse ran up the clock.
The clock struck six!
The mouse, he split.
Hickory Dickory Dock.

Hickory Dickory Dock,
The mouse ran up the clock.
The clock struck seven,
Eight, nine, ten, eleven!
Hickory Dickory Dock.

Hickory Dickory Dock,
The mouse ran up the clock.
As twelve bells rang
The mouse sprang.
Hickory Dickory Dock.

Hickory Dickory Dock,
"Why scamper?" asked the clock.
"You scare me so,
I have to go."
Hickory Dickory Dock.

Pussy Cat, Pussy Cat where have you been?
I've been down to London to see the Queen.
Pussy Cat, Pussy Cat what did you there?
I frightened a little mouse under her chair.

Ding Dong Bell
Pussy's in the well.
Who put her in?
Little Johnny Green.
Who pulled her out?
Little Tommy Stout.
What a naughty boy was that
To try to drown poor pussycat.
Who ne'er did him any harm,
But killed all the mice in the farmer's barn.

I have seen you little mouse
Running all about the house.
Through the hole your little eye
In the wainscot creeping by
Hoping soon some crumbs to steal,
To make quite a hearty meal.
Look before you venture out,
See if pussy is about.

If she's gone you'll quickly run
To the larder for some fun.
Round about the dishes creep,
Taking into each a peep,
To choose the daintiest that's there,
Spoiling things you do not care.

Some little mice
Sat in a barn to spin.
Pussy came by
And popped her head in,
"Shall I come in
And cut your threads off?"
"Oh no, kind sir, you will snap
Our heads off."

One for the mouse,
One for the cow,
One to rot,
One to grow.

WORDS-WORDS-WORDS

People like words but Noah Webster absolutely loved them! He liked words so much he knew more than twenty-seven different languages and was still churning out definitions, pronunciations and spellings of words at the distinguished old age of 70.

Webster published A Compendious Dictionary of the English Language in 1806. By 1844 it had gone into many printings so it truly was compendious. In 1898 the Merriam-Webster Collegiate Dictionary appeared on the scene. Both dictionaries are still being published. Webster noted that a dictionary was the same as a lexicon, a wordbook, or a vocabulary. He might be surprised to find that today the term, 'Webster's', now also means a dictionary. It is an example of how names of products such as 'Kleenex' and 'Scotch Tape' have slipped into our language and are used as generic terms, rather than referring to a particular brand.

In Webster's epony**mouse** Dictionary the word "mouse" is both a noun and a verb. When mouse is a noun it refers to, of course, one of any of those cute little rodents found worldwide. But, hold on, mouse can mean a black eye, a term of endearment, a nautical knot, a match to fire a gun and in recent years a pointing device for a computer. As a verb mouse usually means to hunt for mice or to search for something but sometimes mouse is used to mean to toy with or to move slyly. Mouse has a number of meanings for a one-syllable word.

Webster had fun with words. A mouse-ism is word fun too but so far has not yet made it into a dictionary. Maybe one day it will find its way there. After all, English is a living language and mouse-isms bring new life to old words.

NAUTICAL KNOT

All mice that sail the ocean blue
Need a **mouse** to slip a line through.
Saint Elmouse will always protect
A sailor whose knot is perfect.

MATCH

Unmatched for its' firing ability,
A mouse ignites a **mouse**ket!

COMPUTER MOUSE

While pointing is often impolite,
A computer mouse knows it's quite all right!

BLACK EYE

It's hazardous to hit your eye
For soon a **mouse** bruise you will spy.

TERM OF ENDEARMENT

Such a good sweet little **mouse** you are.
Loved more than any other by far.

TOY WITH

Shake a **Rat**tle and roll.   What fun!

MOUSE HUNT

Looking for something?

GREETING CARDS

Greeting cards have quite a long history. Egyptians exchanged cards made from papyrus and the ancient Chinese enjoyed sending messages of good will at the New Year. Early Europeans sent greeting cards for various holidays. These cards were handmade and quite expensive. The British Museum has on display a Valentine's greeting card from 1400. This card is believed to be the oldest preserved card in existence. Commercial printing in the mid 1850's allowed for cards to be more readily available. Then the emergence of postage stamps and new delivery options furthered the popularity of exchanging cards. Now, in the Twenty-first Century, the card industry realizes billions of dollars a year in business. It is estimated that the average person sends out about fifty-five cards a year.

A card is sent by one person to another for a wide variety of reasons and often can serve multiple purposes. Cards express sentiments and emotions that may be difficult to for a person to articulate. Cards celebrate special occasions such as birthdays, anniversaries, promotions or achievements. Cards convey thoughts of sympathy, of thanks and of hope. Greetings can be humorous or very serious. Today cards come in a wide variety of types. Some cards contain photos and some cards are personalized. Some cards may have tunes operated by a small battery as part of the message while other cards are quite simple and are left blank without a verse inside. Many greetings are sent electronically. The number of reasons a card is sent and the list of types are broad but throughout time the sending of greeting cards has not changed in intention. Greeting cards express care, concern, and thoughts of love and provide that very valuable connection between people.

GET WELL

RATS, I HEARD YOU WERE UNDER THE WEATHER

A mouse had a friend who was not well.
It was hard to decide how to tell
A mouse that was so sick
To get better real quick.
So she sent a note via e-mail

THANK YOU!

MOUSEY BEAUCOUP

There once was a kitten name Sue.
Her ambition? Queen of the Zoo!
She begged and she bothered.
"So Be It!" King hollered.
Sue said sweetly, "**Mouse**y Beaucoup!"

CONGRATULATIONS!

MOUSELTOV!

There once was a **mouse** called Smirnoff
Beer, wine and Scotch were unheard of
He squeaked, "Come on. Celebrate.
Cheese! A **mouse** cannot be late!"
Raise your glasses. Say, "Mouseltov!"

I MADE A MOUSETAKE

I'M SORRY!

There was a **mouse**, a Ramblin' Rake
Blunders for him, a piece of cake,
Wrong. No, not quite right.
Contrite he did write,
"I'm sorry, I made a **mouse**take"

STAY IN TOUCH

Siamouse Twins remain close together
Without a leash or a tether.
No squeaking,
No peeking,
Just two happy birds of a feather.

HAPPY BIRTHDAY!

To honor your birth date
Good tidings are sent.
It's time to celebrate
Such a grand event!

IT MOUSET BE LOVE

As the holiday draws near
It brings all mice good cheer.
A **mouse** is quick you know
To kiss 'neath the mistletoe.

MERRY CHRISTMOUSE

When you hang a shining gold star,
Hang it up on the highest bough.
Let everyone know near and far,
To have a Merry Christmouse now.

Mary Christ**mouse**
Says
Merry Christmas!

ORIGINS AND MEANINGS

Familiar expressions are changed when the word mouse or cat is slyly slipped right into the middle of them. Here is the scuttlebutt on how clichés and sayings have been adapted to mouse terminology in Mouse Word Ho.

Amazon: A Greek word literally meaning, "without a breast". In Greek mythology the Amazons were a nation of warlike women in Asia Minor. Severing off their right breast enabled them to better draw the bow in shooting an arrow.

**Women Warriors Stood Firm And Drew Their Bow
To Win World Wonder Woman Title!**

Cat Nap: This is an expression related to "Playing Cat and Mouse". Cats enjoy playing so when a cat catches a mouse it will then pretend to sleep. The cat, of course, hopes the mouse will try to get away. When the mouse attempts to leave then the cat will have even more fun playing with it.

CAT Scan: C.A.T. is short for X-Ray Computed Axial Tomography. This is also referred to as a C.T. Scan or Computed Tomography. An X-Ray is two-dimensional, but a CAT scan uses digital geometry processing to generate a 3D image. This better image allows medical professionals to gain more detailed information.

A 3D CAT SCAN gives a better picture!

Curiosity Killed the Cat: A woman is called a "cat" especially when she is notably curious, and both spiteful and backbiting. Curiosity killed the Cat stems from an old adage that a cat has nine lives and that only "care will wear them out". Where and when the change in wording occurred turning care into curiosity is not known. The change may reflect wishful thinking. It is rather doubtful anyone held the belief that curiosity would actually kill either a cat or a nosey spiteful woman.

Does it pass the Litmus test? Litmus paper is ancient. It was first used in 1300 A.D. and is the oldest form of testing for pH. Blue litmus paper will turn red under acidic conditions and red litmus paper turns blue under alkaline conditions. This expression has moved out of the chemist's laboratory and into common speech. Its' meaning is to ask if something is real, or true. Does the item in question pass the litmus test?

Doubting Thomas: This is an allusion to Thomas of the Bible who was one of the twelve apostles. He refused to believe it was Christ who had risen from the dead until he, Thomas, had felt the wounds.

Handicap: A word originating from the procedure of drawing lots. Slips of paper were placed in a cap. Each person in turn drew his place for the race by placing his "hand in cap". Today the term is better known to refer to a disadvantage imposed on a superior competitor or to an allowance given an inferior competitor.

Handkerchief: "Kerchief" comes from the old French words "covir" and "ker" meaning to cover and from "chief" meaning head. Originally a kerchief was a head covering. Women used a kerchief when entering a Roman Catholic Church. A handkerchief therefore was the kerchief that was carried in her hand.

Hat Trick: A hat trick describes the act of one player achieving three goals or three feats in a single game. It was first used in 1859 in cricket when the player, H.H. Stephenson, took three wickets in three balls. A collection taken up to honor him was given to him in a hat. The term went on to be adapted to all sports but it is most commonly used in the sport of ice hockey.

Missouri: Missouri's nickname, "The Show Me State" comes from an expression popularized by Congressman Willard Vandiver in speech he made in 1899. In this speech Vandiver said that he was from a country that grew corn and cotton as crops and he was not impressed by "frothy elegance". He said, "I'm from Missouri and you'll have to show me". Researchers date the expression a little further back to the early 1890's and to the mining town, Leadville, Colorado. Men migrated to Colorado to get work by replacing striking miners. As these men were new to the job and needed training the mining boss was said to have to constantly repeat, "That man is from Missouri. You'll have to show him."

Mother Earth: At one time it was thought that earth was the "mother" of all the peoples of the world.

Mother-of-Pearl: A pearl grows and develops out of and as a part of the inner lining of the mollusks' shell. This inner lining is therefore called, "mother-of-pearl". Mother-of-pearl is strong, resilient and iridescent. It is used in architecture, fashion, musical instruments and jewelry.

Muscle: The word muscle is derived from Latin, musculus, and means little mouse. The term was used because the way the muscles of the upper arm move resemble the action of a mouse crawling back and forth.

Poor as a Church Mouse: This expression has been referenced as early as the 17th Century and likely descriptive of conditions in early times. Old stone churches and cathedrals were unheated and cold. The sacristy would have perhaps a drop of consecrated wine and a few crumbs left from the bread or wafer used in the Eucharist. Without heat and without food a church mouse was very poor indeed.

Raining Cats and Dogs: This is from Norse mythology. The cat symbolizes heavy rain. The dog, an attendant of Odin, represents great blasts of wind. Traditionally cats and dogs are portrayed to be great enemies so they were used to represent the elements of conflict in a storm.

Red Herring (Yarmouth capon): A Yarmouth capon is a fish more commonly known as a red herring. "It's a red herring" is an expression that refers to the attempt to distract attention from the main issue. A red herring, after curing, has a pungent odor. When a red herring is dragged across a fox hunting trail the smell can distract the dogs or fox hounds. The hounds will follow the trail of the red herring instead of the fox.

Siamese Twins: Conjoined twins are frequently referred to as Siamese Twins. The first conjoined twins to be exhibited throughout the world were Chang and Eng, twin brothers born in Siam. These men, joined at the waist, lived a full life. They married two sisters, and lived out their lives as farmers in North Carolina. Chang had six children and Eng had five.

Taxi: Taxi comes from the meter carried by a cab. It was originally called a taximeter because it measured the fare or the 'tax'. Cabs in the mid to late 1890's that were equipped with these meters advertised the fact by painting "Taximeter" on the cab doors. Taximeter was quickly shortened to Taxi.

Turnpike: Toll highways get their name from the poles or bars called "pikes" which were swung on a pivot across a road in the 17th Century. These pikes had to be turned before any vehicle or carriage or a man on horseback could pass. The pikes were set up along the road to ensure the collection of the tolls on the highway. One of the first turnpikes established was on the Great North Road in England in 1663.

Under the Weather: When on a sailing vessel a person subject to seasickness could seek shelter from the wind by crouching down beside the bulwarks. This put the person "under" the bulwark's protection, which was on the "weather" or the windy side of the ship.

X-Ray: At first this ray was called the "Roentgen Ray" in honor of the scientist who discovered it. The letter, X, an algebraic symbol for the unknown, is what Roentgen preferred to call his discovery. This was because at that time, Roentgen himself did not fully understand the nature of the ray.

X-RATED MOUSE

**Only adult mice are allowed to see this picture.
Clearly, she is not P.G.**

CRAFTY MICE

The Clever Mouse

Scraps, Crafts. Spins and Sews

CRAFTY MICE

Now here's a small yarn to spin
Of mice that know how to win
A stitch here or there.
Superglue needed where?
Nothing here can be made of tin.

Many mice can do many things
They are crafty and clever it seems.
They don't like to tease
Look inside, if you please,
For art forms that will surely bring beams.

First, there's sleepy baby so small
With a wee cry to notify all.
Handy Hanky—Candy Mouse,
Your doubts they will douse.
Crafty items do make life a ball.

A CANDY CANE MOUSE

Candy canes are a common sight at the holidays. The legend is that in the mid-1600's the **choirmousester** at the Cologne Cathedral in Germany handed out sugar sticks bent into the shape of a shepherd's staff to his young singers. These sugary sticks were designed to keep the children quiet during long services. Later, in the mid-1800's in Wooster, Ohio, August Imgard began to use candy canes as a tree decoration.

Here is just one of several patterns for making a mouse out of felt and a candy cane. Supplies needed are felt in any color or combination of colors, a candy cane and plastic eyes or buttons. For a more permanent ornament plastic candy canes can be purchased at craft or dollar stores.

Trace or copy the templates to make patterns. From the patterns cut a body and ears from felt. The body and ears can be one color or of two colors for interest. A gray mouse with pink ears or perhaps a green mouse with red ears would make a statement. Where indicated on the template pattern cut two slits in the felt body piece. Slip the ears through these two slits. They will scrunch easily.

On the backside of the mouse thread either a real candy cane or a plastic candy cane through the center of the earpiece. If desired, put a dab of glue between the felt and the candy cane to hold it in place. Turn the mouse over and glue or sew on buttons or little goggle eyes.
Hang the mouse by its' tail!

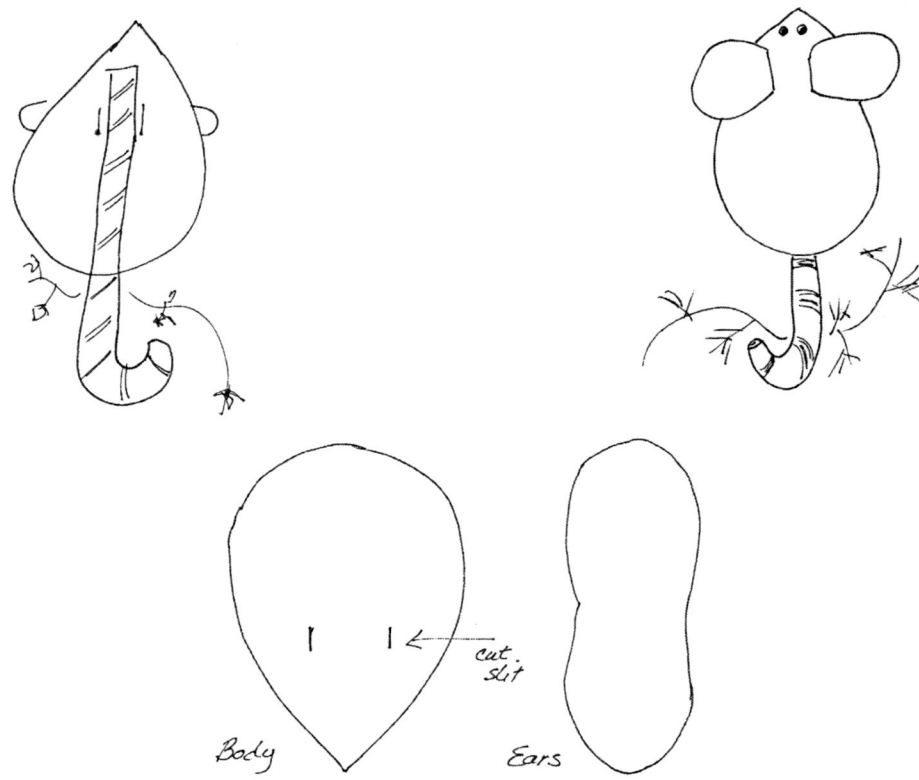

ARTIFICIAL FRUIT MICE

Needed to make this mouse is any type of artificial fruit that has a stem. Strawberries are very nice but apples and pears will work well. Also needed are scraps of felt, craft eyes or paint, and craft wire.
Select a piece of artificial fruit and put it on a working surface. If the fruit is too rounded it might wobble a bit. If this is so, gently slice off one side of the fruit to make a short flat edge. This flat edge will form the base of the mouse and keep it from rolling or tipping to one side.

Turn the fruit so that the stem is in the position for the mouse's tail. With the mouse now facing you, paint or attach small googly-eyes or beads for eyes. Cut scraps of felt into two pear shapes. Attach these to the mouse for its' ears. Take short lengths of craft wire and thread the wire straight across the nose. Do this with two or three pieces of wire to form whiskers.

An artificial fruit mouse is perfect for gracing a cheese board as it can easily be washed and cleaned (See Cheese Please). A magnet may be attached to the mouse's 'belly' base for use as a refrigerator décor.

EASY TO SEW SLEEPY BABY FABRIC MOUSE

Get out the sewing mouse-chine! It is easy to create a small fabric mouse. A fabric mouse can be made in any size desired. Use felt, a scrap of print cotton fabric, cotton balls or a bit of batting, ribbon and small beads.

Start by cutting a piece of felt into the shape of a house. For a small mouse use a piece of felt about 2 ½ inches by 2 inches. Fold it in half and then on the long side measure up one inch. Cut across from that point to the center of the top. This will create a long triangle at one end of the felt and a rectangular shape at the other end. Keeping this house shape folded, stitch along the two cut edges on the long angled side. Stuff the stitched body with a bit of cotton batting or use a shredded cotton ball. Now stitch across the shorter bottom edge to close the mouse up. Add two beads at each side of the head for eyes.

Cut a small piece of colored or print fabric into a rectangle that is about twice as long as the body of the mouse. For the above size mouse use a piece of fabric 3 1/4 inches long by 4 inches wide. Make a pillow-case. Start by stitching a hem along the long edge of the rectangle. Fold the rectangle in half with right sides together. Align the stitched hem. Stitch together the two cut edges. Turn right side out. This little bag will be the mouse's blanket.

Put the felt mouse into its' fabric blanket, just like a sleeping bag. Tie a narrow 1/8 in. ribbon around the top. Dot the ribbon with fabric glue to hold it in place.

Line up many mice to make a display. Tuck a fabric mouse into a blouse or a shirt pocket for a cute conversation piece. Attach a mouse to a key ring and carry it for good luck. Can a fabric mouse go to school in a child's lunch bag or box?

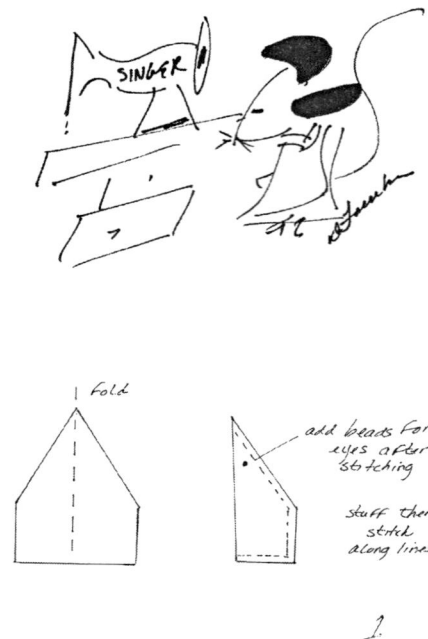

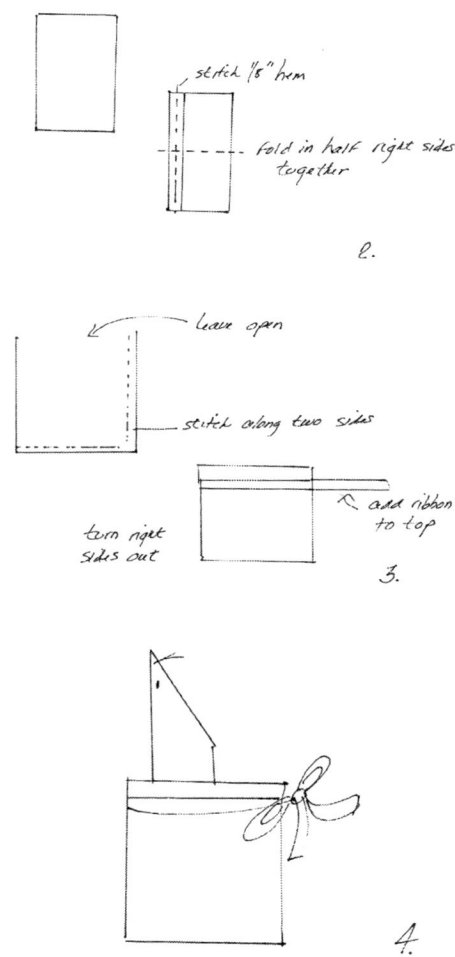

HANDY HANKY MOUSE

Years ago, before disposable tissues became common, handkerchiefs were used universally. Handkerchiefs were usually either linen or cotton squares. Almost everyone carried one. Hankies were used to wipe hands, blot sweat from a brow and of course to wipe a runny nose or capture a sneeze. Children found a hanky useful to carry small items in. Women used a hanky to carry coins. Handkerchiefs, knotted at the four corners, have even been used to protect a baldhead from the sun. Hankies are definitely handy.

Folding a hanky, or a napkin, into specific objects is an interesting old custom. Generations of adults have fashioned a doll or a little mouse out of a hanky. These creations were meant to entertain young ones and were especially useful when children were expected to be quiet or to be those children who were to be " seen and not heard".

Try to make a Handy Hanky Mouse. Some people like to try and make a hanky mouse "jump" by putting the mouse on the top of one arm and stroking it with the other hand. This makes the little hanky mouse jump a bit in the air. There are videos available on the Internet that can give additional help in making a mouse out of a hanky.

How to Make a Handy Hanky Mouse

Begin with a square fabric handkerchief or napkin.
Lay the hanky on a flat surface so it is in the shape of a diamond.

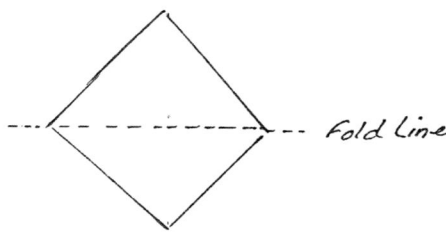

Fold it up to create a triangle. Fold both side points of the triangle over to the center. It will look like the shape of an envelope.

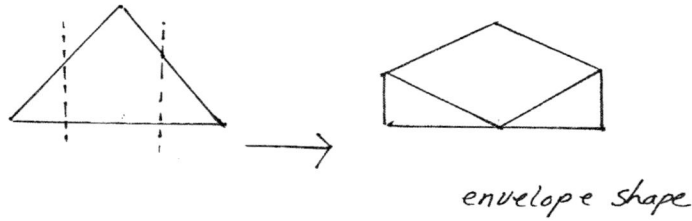

Roll up the bottom edge of the hanky towards the point. Stop just before the roll hits the point. Turn the hanky over.

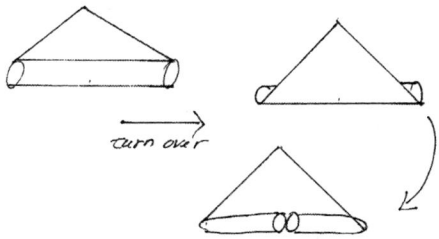

Fold in each end of the rolled portion to the center.
Fold the ends of the triangle points over these to create a donut shape.

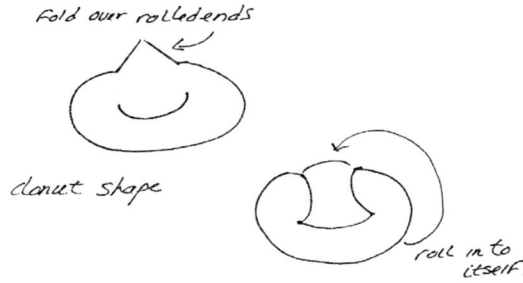

Roll the round donut into itself. One side of the roll will feel a little fatter than the other side. Continue rolling until the points poke back out again at either side.

Pull out one point and open it up into a diamond shape. Fold the top corner over to create small triangle. Tie both ends into a small knot. The center of the knot becomes the mouse's head and the little corners are its ears.

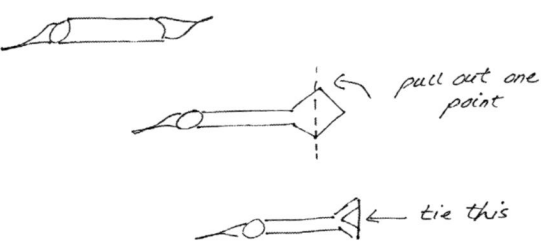

Leave one triangle point out for the tail Twist it in on itself to make it a skinny tail.

PAPER MOUSE

A mouse can be made out of any kind of paper. Plain bond paper, gift-wrap, newspaper or double-sided scrapbook paper can all be used. Start by cutting a four-inch circle out of the paper that has been selected. Take the circle and gently fold it in half. Do not crease it. Take this half circle and turn down the upper end about one third of the way from the top. Make a small cut at the side of the fold. Open the circle up.
Cut two round ears. Roll or fold the base of one ear and slip it into a slit. Do the same with the second ear. On the wrong side of the paper put a small piece of cellophane tape to secure both ears.

Turn the paper to the right side and form it into a cone shape. Tape the edge. Uncurl the ears if necessary.

Cut a 1/4 inch wide piece of paper about six-inches long and taper it to form a long narrow triangle. Attach a piece of tape to the wider end and slide it into the cone and tape it down to make a tail.

Draw beady eyes with a black pen or marker.
A paper mouse is disposable. It makes an excellent place card and can be an adornment for a gift package or for a food tray. Instructions are for a small mouse but other sizes can easily be made following the same guidelines. Paper mice make a good craft project for kids.

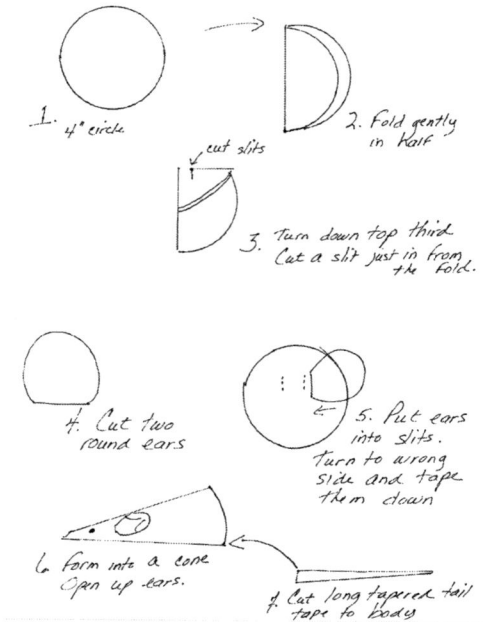

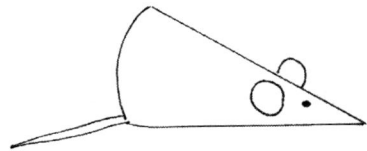

TUSSIE-MOUSE-SIE

A Mouse Nosegay

An herbal tussie-mouse-sie will provide hours of enjoyment. It could give a hospitalized friend a lift in spirits to have a delightful fragrance nearby. It can make a thoughtful bon voyage gift, or an ideal dinner favor. When dried, a tussie-mouse-sie will still remain fragrant for months.

♦ Choose any large flower for the center. Use a rose or a daisy or a mum.
♦ Add to this single flower two or three sprigs of fragrant herbs. Try using flowering herbs such as oregano or thyme. Frame these flowering herbs with other herbs such as tansy, violet or lambs' ear. The nosegay can also include mint or rosemary leaves for additional fragrance.
♦ Bind the stems together with string and tie off. Do not damage the stems by pulling the string too tightly. Trim the stems of any uneven ends. Lace, a pretty ribbon or a paper doily can then be used to cover the string tie.
♦ Put the tussie-mouse-sie in bud vase or little container with water.

Give a tussie-mouse-ie to a special someone sending all
your best wishes with it.

AUTHOR'S NOTE

Thirty years ago Denine Foulks and Joann Dettmann met at Misawa Air Base, Japan where both of their husbands were serving as officers in The United States Air Force. Joann was the editor of the Officer's Wives Club newsletter, The Torii Times and Denine pitched in with a few drawings. Joann's idea of making up a Misawa Mouse coupled with Denine's drawings of one quickly blossomed and led to many hours of laughter as mouse-isms were created.

In 1986 Joann made a concerted effort to have a Mouse Word Dictionary published. Later in 2006 Denine entered the world of greeting cards. Eventually these ideas and concepts merged and Mouse Word Ho was the result.

It is a gift to have had many years of laughter, fun and friendship. The authors thank their husbands and families for their love, encouragement and of course for the mouse-isms they have all thrown in for good measure.

The End of A Mouse-story

ABOUT THE AUTHORS

Denine Foulks is an RN Consultant. She has published two family heritage cookbooks. Denine enjoys quilting, sewing projects, and crafts. She currently sings in a 100-voice chorus and studies piano. She and her husband divide their time between New Hampshire and South Carolina.

Joann Dettmann is an RN who worked in geriatric nursing for many years and now does contract work for health fairs and flu clinics. She has had articles published in Ski Magazine and several military, church and community publications. She and her husband reside in Virginia.

CPSIA information can be obtained at www.ICGtesting.com
Printed in the USA
LVOW080252051012

301596LV00004B/6/P